The Avalans shut their doors and lit their fires. Almost no one saw the black ships that sailed silently into the harbour . . .

. . . or the strangers who leapt ashore,

snuck through the streets,

seized the city,

and captured the prince.

They took him far away and hid him in a fortress in the heart of the island.

Locked in the dark for days, the prince lost all hope.

But then, one night, he saw his chance.

The prince ran . . .

. . . and ran.

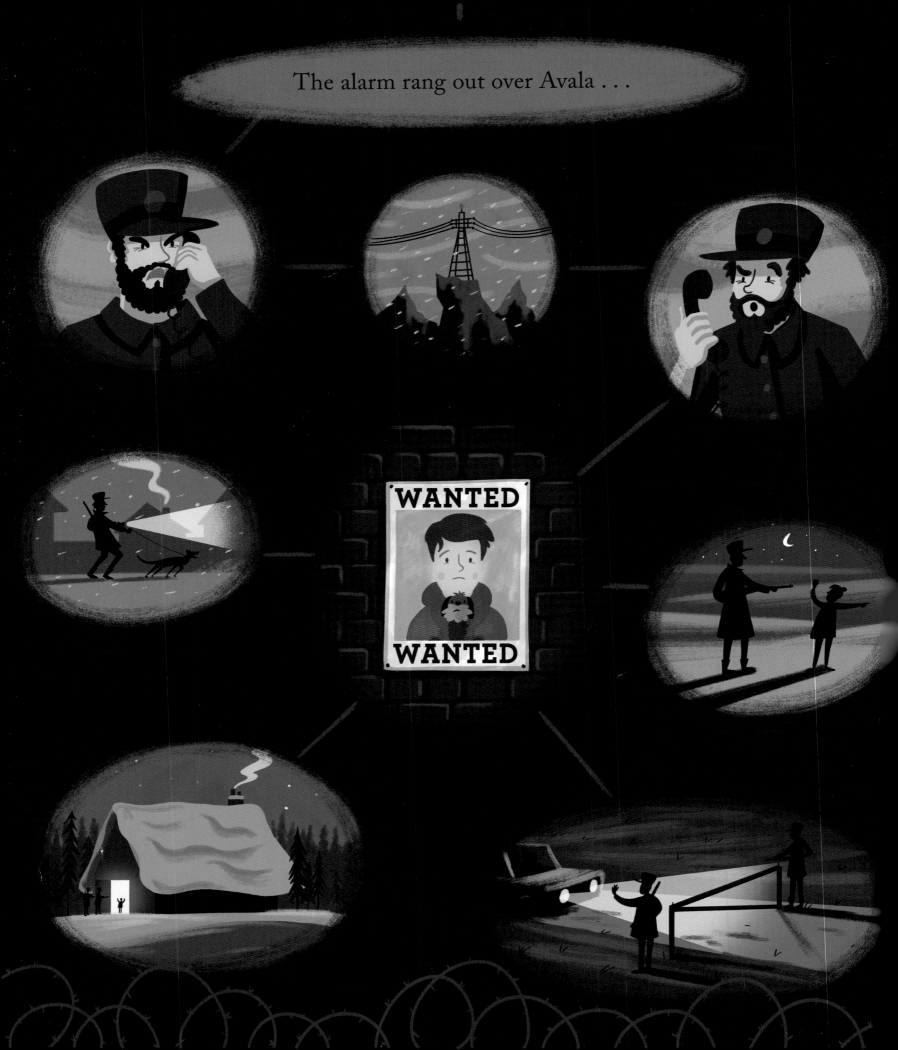

. . . and soon the island was crawling with strangers,
all searching for the little red prince.

He stumbled through the snow, until he saw
the flickering light of a fire.

A young girl sat beside the flames.
"You have to get to the city," she told him.
"Your friends are waiting for you."
"But how will I get there?" asked the prince.
"The strangers are everywhere."
"Don't worry," she said. "You'll find help in
the most unexpected places."

As the prince made his way across the island . . .

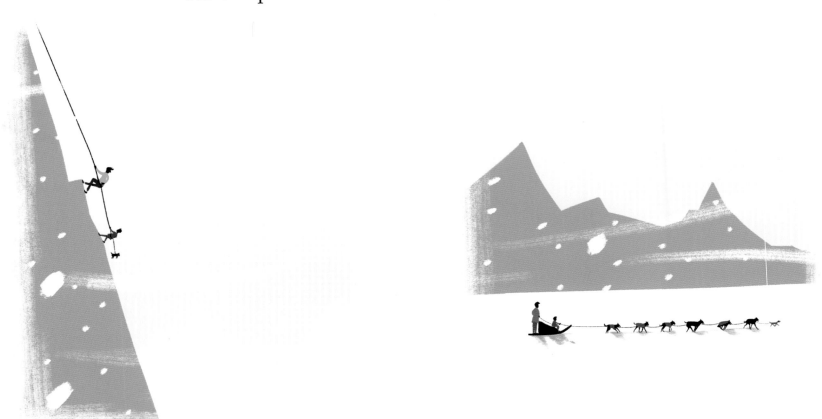

. . . he found that the girl was right!

The Avalans did everything they could to
confuse and confound the strangers . . .

. . . and the red prince was able to sneak all the
way to the city gates.

He could hear a great commotion from behind the walls,
but saw no way past the guards . . .

. . . when suddenly they were distracted,

and he slipped inside.

There, he saw something
he couldn't believe.

All of Avala were dressed as red princes! The city was filled with ruby red and rang with laughter and music.

The prince danced through the streets for hours, invisible in a sea of brilliant colour.

Until he left the safety of the crowd.

The strangers chased him down,

but the prince was no longer afraid . . .

The strangers scrabbled to their boats, rowed to their
ship, and sailed away from the island of Avala.

Never to return.

Chirp, chirp, churr, churr, buzz, buzz, whirr, whirr.

树叶沙沙，吊床摇摆。孩子们在玩耍。

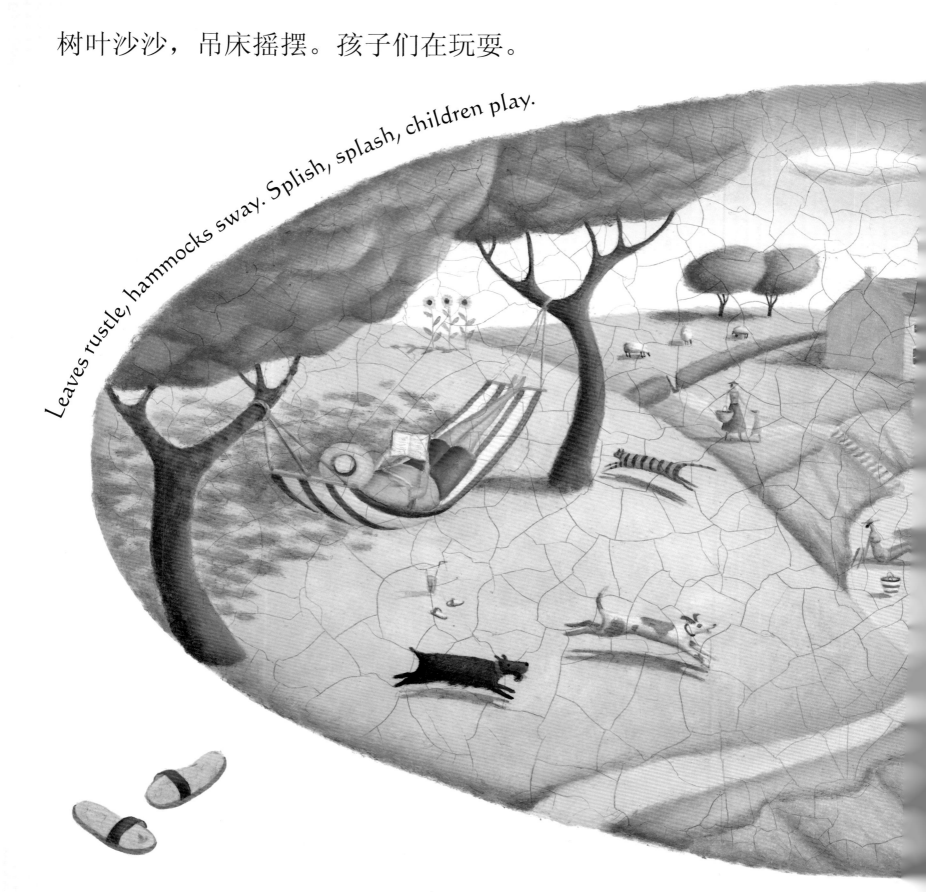

Leaves rustle, hammocks sway. Splish, splash, children play.

浮云飘动，狗儿奔跑。哧哧，哧哧，夏日阳光在闪耀。

Clouds drift, dogs run. Sizzle, sizzle, summer sun.

听，听... 夏天走了。再见小虫子，秋天来了。

Listen, listen ... summer's gone.
Good-bye insects, autumn's come.

扑通，扑通，橡子掉落。快啊，松鼠跳跃。

Plop, plop, acorns drop.
Hurry, scurry, squirrels hop.

快啊，快啊，南瓜熟了。收割玉米，摘苹果啦。

Pumpkins ripen, quick, quick. Apples, corn - pick, pick.

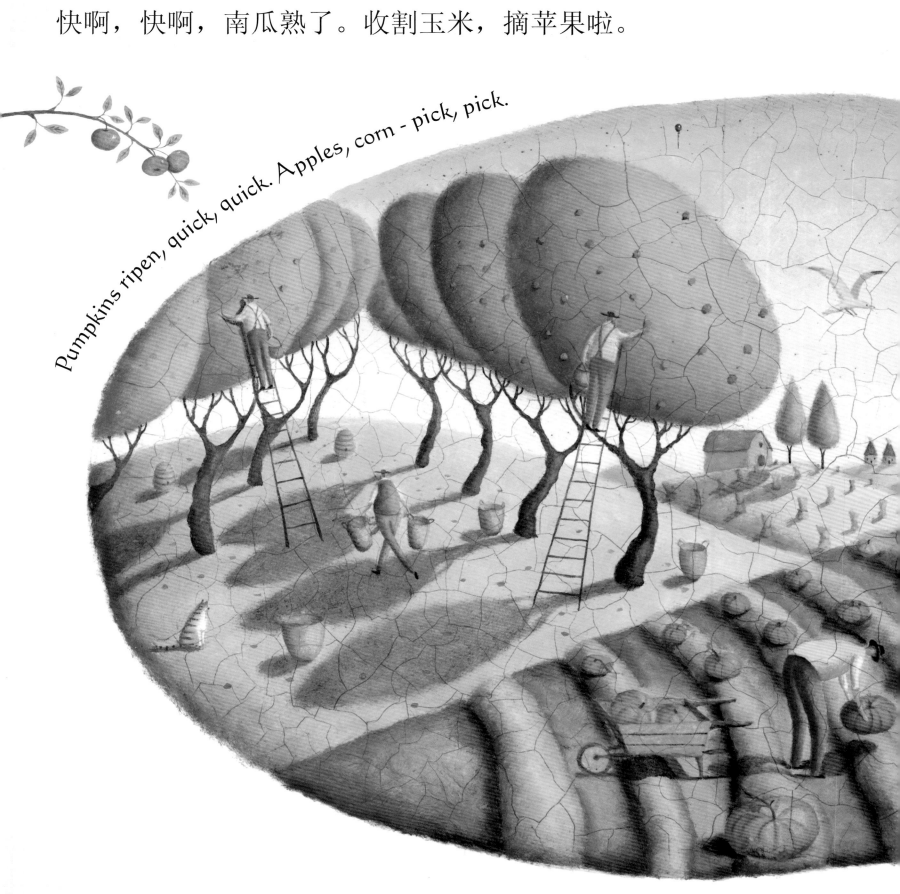

嘎嚓，嘎嚓，人们走动。嗷嗷，嗷嗷，海鸥鸣叫。

欧欧，欧欧，大雁鸣叫。嗖嗖，嗖嗖，树叶坠落。

Honk, honk, geese call. Swish, swish, leaves fall.

嗖嗖，嗖嗖，帽子飞翔。呼呼，呼呼，猫头鹰哭泣。

*Whoosh, whoosh, hats fly. Whoo, whoo, owls cry.*

听，听... 秋天走了。雪花低语，'冬天很有趣'。

Listen, listen ... autumn's gone. Snowflakes whisper, "Winter's fun."

嘘，嘘，多雪的夜晚。雪花闪烁，洁白闪亮。

Shhh, shhh, snowy night. Snow sparkles, white, bright.

嘎嚓，嘎嚓，靴子踏步。铁锹挥动，孩子们嬉戏。

Crunch, crunch, boots clomp. Grown-ups shovel, children romp.

溜冰者旋转，滑雪者滑翔。上升，滑动，旋转飞舞。

Skaters spin, skiers glide. Zip, zoom, slip, slide.

啊啊，哦哦，热身时间。嚯嚯，嗬嗬，蜡烛闪耀。

*Brrr, brrr, warm-up time. Ooh, aah, candles shine.*

咕噜，咕噜，猫咪凝视。劈啪，劈啪，火焰燃烧。

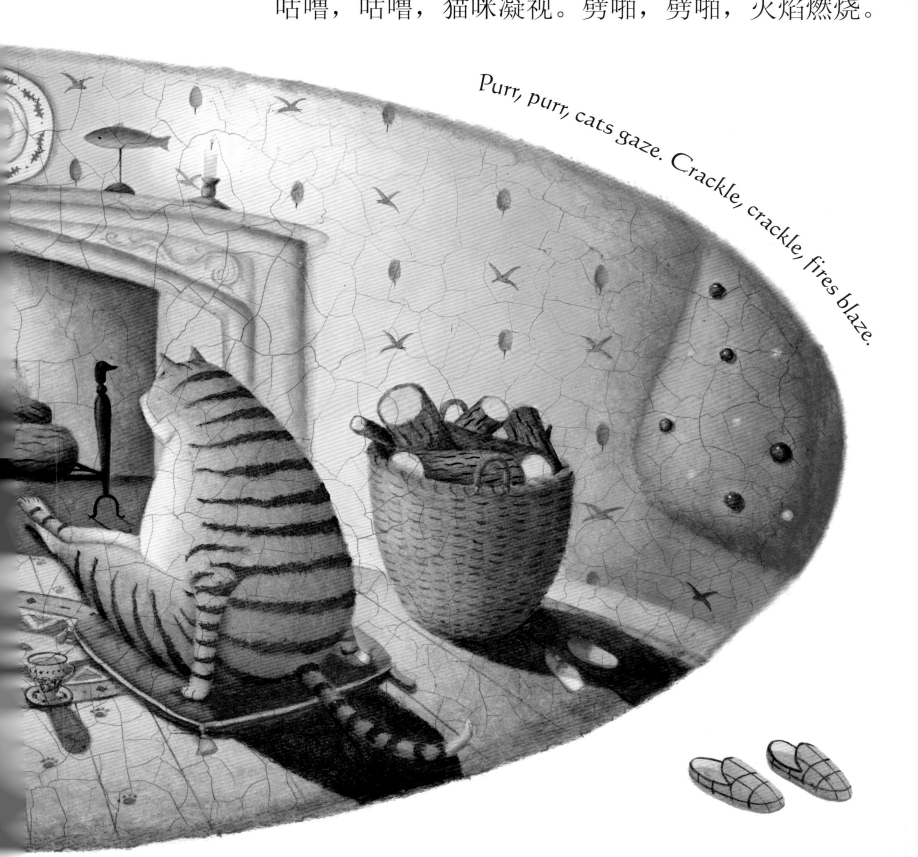

Purr, purr, cats gaze. Crackle, crackle, fires blaze.

听，听... 冬天走了。鸟儿鸣叫，'这里有阳光！'

Listen, listen ... winter's gone. Finches whistle, "Here's the sun!"

砰砰，砰砰，球茎萌芽。树叶生长，花儿呐喊。

Pop, pop, bulbs sprout. Leaves grow, flowers shout.

劈啪，劈啪，婴儿诞生。偷看，偷看，小鸡刨地。

Crick, crack, babies hatch. Peep, peep, chickens scratch.

青蛙呱呱，小鸭子呷呷。小兔子用力咀嚼。

Frogs croak, ducklings quack. Munch, munch, rabbits snack.

啪嗒，啪嗒，雨珠落下。啾啾，啾啾，麻雀聚集。

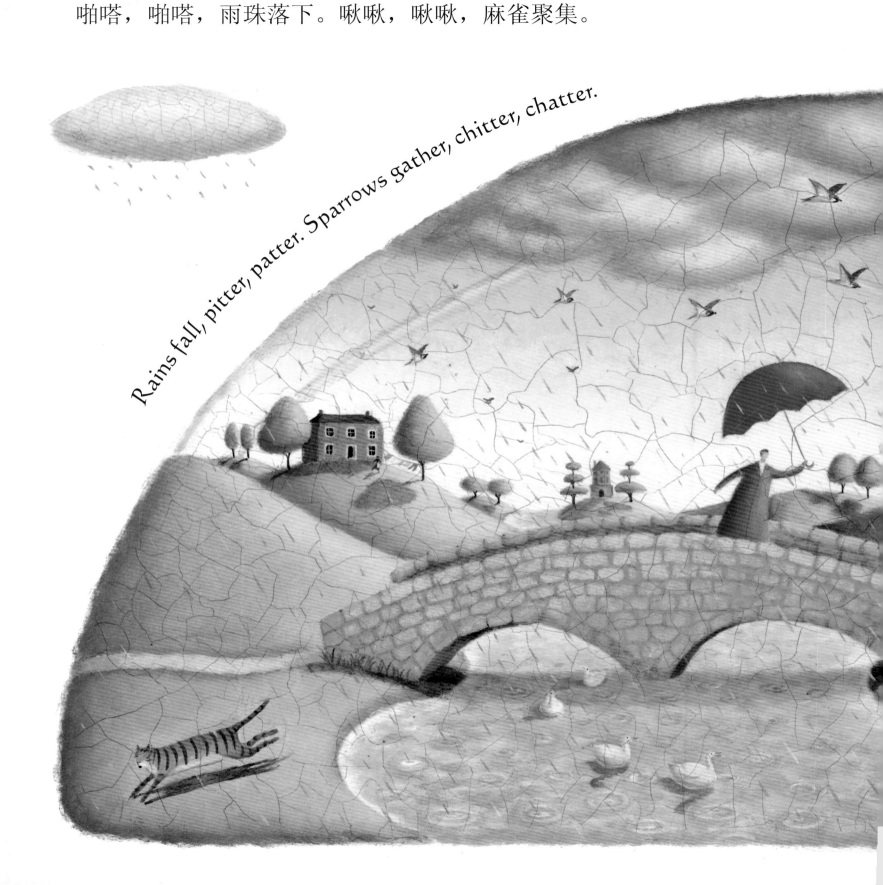

Rains fall, pitter, patter. Sparrows gather, chitter, chatter.

听，听... 春天走了。新的季节开始了。

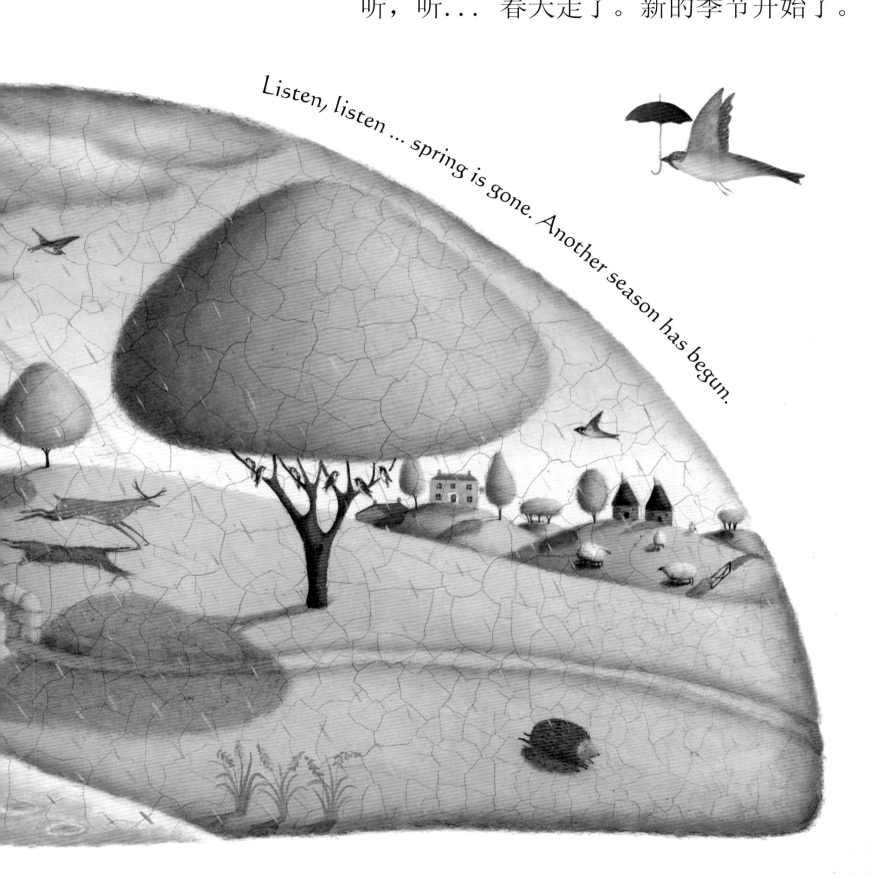

Listen, listen ... spring is gone. Another season has begun.

在空中，在地上，白天和黑夜... 这是什么声音？

In the air, on the ground, night and day - what's that sound?

听，听... 春天过后，夏天来了。

Listen, listen ... after spring, summer comes and ...

昆虫歌唱。

Insects sing!

叽叽，喳喳，嗡嗡，呼呼。

Chirp, chirp, churr, churr, buzz, buzz, whirr, whirr.

In the summer, can you see

a cricket

a butterfly

a mosquito

a bee

a dragonfly

a grasshopper

a beetle

a sunflower

a daisy

a leaf?

In the autumn, can you see

an owl

a goose

an acorn

an apple

a squirrel

a stalk of wheat

a pumpkin

an ear of corn

a seagull

a leaf?

In the winter, can you see

a crow

a mouse

a starling

a paw print

a holly berry

an icicle

a snowflake

a leaf?

a sprig of mistletoe

In the spring, can you see

a tulip

a frog

a daffodil

a duckling

a bluebell

a chick

a rainbow

a rabbit

a sparrow

a leaf?

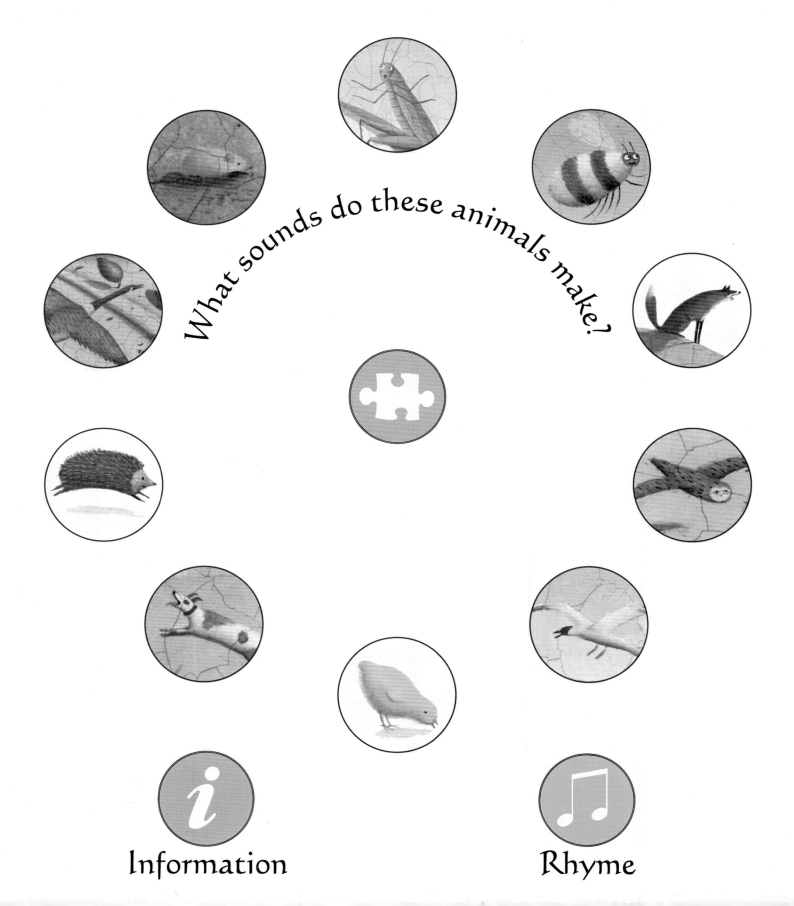

What sounds do these animals make?

Information

Rhyme